AMY WU and the PATCHWORK DRAGON

For Michael, who always believes —K. Z.

For everyone who loves Amy Wu! —C. C.

SIMON & SCHUSTER BOOKS FOR YOUNG READERS • An imprint of Simon & Schuster Children's Publishing Division • 1230 Avenue of the Americas, New York, New York 10020

• For information about special discounts for bulk purchases, please contact Simon & Schuster Special Sales at 1-866-506-1949 or business@simonandschuster.com. • The Simon & Schuster Speakers Bureau can bring authors to your live event. For more information or to book an event contact the Simon & Schuster Speakers Bureau at 1-866-248-3049 or visit our website at www.simonspeakers.com. • Designed by Laura Lyn DiSiena
The illustrations for this book were rendered digitally. • The text of this book was set in Andes Rounded. • Manufactured in China • 0920 SCP • First Edition • 10 9 8 7 6 5 4 3 2 1
CIP data for this book is available from the Library of Congress. • ISBN 9781534463639 (hc) • ISBN 9781534463646 (eBook)

By
KAT ZHANG

Illustrated by
CHARLENE CHUA

SIMON & SCHUSTER BOOKS FOR YOUNG READERS
New York London Toronto Sydney New Delhi

During story time, Ms. Mary reads Amy's class a book about **dragons**.

Dragons that hoard **treasure**.

Dragons that blow **fire**.

Dragons that fight knights
in **gleaming armor**.

Afterward, she tells everyone to make their own dragons.

"Make them special!" she says.

"Make them **yours**."

Sam draws a dragon with **enormous teeth**.
He crafts the wings from postage stamps.

Willa sculpts a dragon with a big, **fat belly**. She strings daisies for the tail.

Amy paints a dragon with a long, thin body. It has **horns** like a stag and **claws** like an eagle.

“Are you sure that’s a dragon?” asks Sam.

“It doesn’t **look** like a dragon,” adds Willa.

"Hmm . . . ," Amy says.

Maybe they're right.

Amy scribbles with her pencil and doodles with her crayons. She glues beads to the paper (and some to her hair).

Bits of dragons emerge. Dragons with shiny green scales. Dragons with leathery wings. They look great. They look just like the dragons in Ms. Mary's book. But . . .

None of them work. None of them feel quite right.

These dragons are **not** the dragons Amy wanted to make.

“Time to clean up!” says Ms. Mary.

“I’m not done!” cries Amy.

The rest of the class put their dragons on the show-and-tell table.

But there's **nothing** from Amy.

Nothing at all.

Willa and Sam come over after school, but Amy can't even smile.

"Oh dear," says Amy's grandma. "Why the sad face?"

So Amy tells her.

Her grandma gets a **twinkle** in her eye.

"Come," she says.
"Let me tell you a story."

She tells them about
dragons that bring
down the rain.

Dragons that are
wise and just.

Dragons that fly without wings.

Amy runs to the attic. She remembers where she got the idea for her dragon!

She pulls out something red and yellow. Something with a big, fat snout and golden horns . . .

"A dragon!" gasp Sam and Willa.

"A dragon," agrees Amy.

Amy's grandma puts on the costume's head, and Amy puts on the tail.

Together, they dance down the attic steps
and roar through the house.

"Maybe you can
bring it to school,"
says Sam.

“Please, **please** bring it to school,” begs Willa.

“Hmm . . . ,” says Amy.

She thinks about the dragons in Ms. Mary's book.

She thinks about the dragons in Grandma's story.

Bringing this dragon to class would be great, but . . .

there's something missing.

Something to make the dragon **Amy's**.

After Sam and Willa go home, Amy begins to plan.

She shows her sketches to her family.

"Will you help me?"

she asks.

They measure out fabric and cut it into shape. They carve a cardboard frame and fasten the cloth.

Amy knots together three silk scarves.

Then she adds some beads.

And some glitter . . .

and a little more glitter, just because.

“Ready?” asks Grandma.

Amy takes a deep breath.

“Ready,” she says.

Amy comes to school with a
big paper bag.

The other children gather around.

"Is it your dragon?" asks Willa.
"Show us!" cries Sam.

Amy puts on the dragon's head. She invites
Willa and Sam beneath the dragon's tail.

Together, they dance through the classroom and roar between the desks. Everybody cheers. Ms. Mary laughs so hard, she can't even breathe.

Amy's dragon is red and yellow. It has a big, fat snout and golden horns. It has enormous green wings and a tail of three silk scarves.

And **beads**.

And **glitter**.

Lots of glitter.

It works splendidly.

It feels just right.

It is **exactly** the dragon Amy wanted to make.

Aa
Bb
CHEETAH

DRAGON ACTIVITY

Please make sure a grown-up helps you with this craft activity. Have fun!

MAKE YOUR VERY OWN DRAGON!

YOU WILL NEED:
Tracing paper
Construction paper*
Scissors
Split pins
Art supplies for decorating your dragon

1. Have a grown-up help you trace the dragon body pieces on the following pages, and cut them out.
2. Use the tracing-paper cutouts to trace the body pieces onto construction paper, and cut out your final pieces. You can reuse the tracing-paper cutouts multiple times.
3. Use split pins to attach the pieces together and make a unique dragon that's all your own!
4. Color and decorate your dragon with crayons, colored pencils, markers, paints, or other art supplies! (Amy particularly likes glitter and beads.)

**Extra ideas: Feel free to replace the construction paper with foam sheets, thin cardboard, card stock, etc. This will create sturdier dragons, but you may need to pre-poke a hole for the split pins.*

EASTERN DRAGON

The Eastern dragon is a symbol of good luck and strength in many cultures! It usually has a long, thin body and no wings. Its horns look like stag antlers, and its claws look like eagle claws. Its body is covered in scales. Eastern dragons come in many different colors and can have a wide range of magic powers, depending on the story. Often, they are very intelligent.

WESTERN DRAGON

Western dragons usually have four legs and one pair of big, leathery wings. Like Eastern dragons, their bodies are covered in scales. Unlike Eastern dragons, they often breathe fire! Stories about Western dragons tend to show them as greedy creatures that live in caves and love treasure. Their horns tend to be sharp and pointy, and their claws look like lizard claws.